D1441227

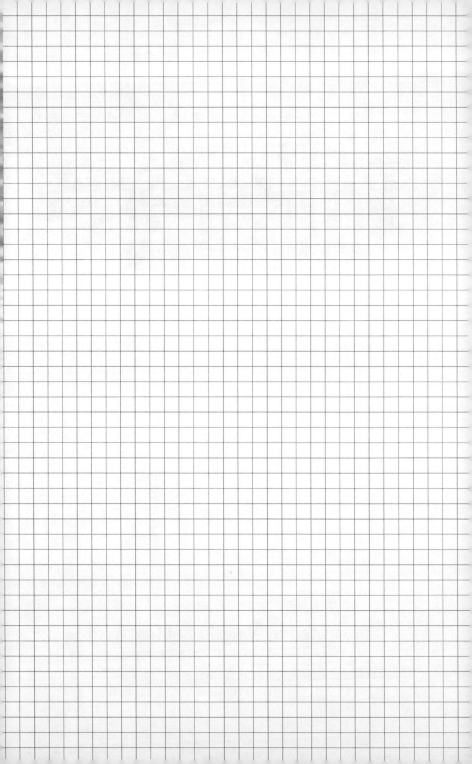

The Tinkerers
FORCES OF NATURE

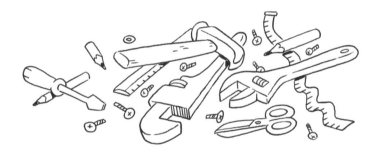

Patricia Lakin

illustrated by Valerio Fabbretti

Albert Whitman & Company
Chicago, Illinois

For my father, Samuel Miller Lakin,
an inspirational tinkerer, par excellence.
With enormous thanks to our son, Benjahmin,
an imaginative tinkerer.—PL

To my grandparents—VF

Library of Congress Cataloging-in-Publication
data is on file with the publisher.

Text copyright © 2022 by Patricia Lakin
Illustrations copyright © 2022 by Albert Whitman & Company
Illustrations by Valerio Fabbretti
First published in the United States of America
in 2022 by Albert Whitman & Company

ISBN 978-0-8075-7953-4 (hardcover)
ISBN 978-0-8075-7954-1 (ebook)

Printed in the United States of America
10 9 8 7 6 5 4 3 2 1 LB 26 25 24 23 22 21

Design by Aphelandra

For more information about Albert Whitman & Company,
visit our website at www.albertwhitman.com.

CONTENTS

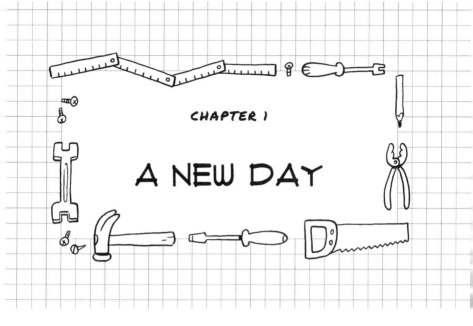

CHAPTER 1

A NEW DAY

Roscoe opened one eye. Then the other. A new day! He hoped the storm had finally ended. For two days, rain had poured down around the shed he called home.

"Quiet, you," Roscoe said to his growling belly. But he knew the truth. As with any raccoon, Roscoe's stomach ruled. When it needed food, there was no way of stopping it. Well, almost no way. Roscoe *never* went out in a rainstorm.

As he yawned and stretched, Roscoe gazed up at the drawings he'd made while stuck inside. The

1

first was a sketch of his latest idea—a mechanical arm that allowed him to create two drawings at the same time. He'd already created a pop-up toast catcher.

But today, Roscoe looked longingly at the drawing he'd made of his favorite food—a slice of pizza sprinkled with tuna fish and pickles. His food drawing almost looked real. But it was, after all, only a drawing. It didn't satisfy his hunger one bit.

So Roscoe climbed out of his cozy, warm bed. He shuffled to the window in his cozy, warm shed.

"No rain!" he said, patting his belly. "You'll be full soon."

That meant a trip down the hill, across the river, and straight to his favorite food source. The sign on the fence's gate called the place "Sparkling Meadow Recycling Center." But that was just a fancy name for what the humans did there.

Really, it was where they dumped their stuff. One thing they dumped they called "garbage."

That was *not* what Roscoe called it. He called it breakfast, lunch, and dinner.

Grumble! Growl!

"I'm moving as quickly as I can," Roscoe told his belly as he put on his trusty vest. He unzipped

one pocket and slipped in his drawing pencils. He unzipped another pocket and slipped in his spectacles. Then he unzipped the biggest pocket of all. That was where Roscoe kept his drawing pad.

Outside, Roscoe whistled as he walked. He passed by mountains of stoves and rows of refrigerators. He scooted around car doors piled high. He jumped over rain puddles as he passed bins of instruments, plugs, wires, and hinges.

The rusty sign on the fence of Roscoe's home called it "Big River Junkyard." But Roscoe knew that wasn't right either. What humans liked to call "junk" was much more to him. As an artist and inventor, Roscoe had all the supplies he needed to build anything his brain could come up with.

Roscoe crouched down so he could slide through the opening under the fence. In a few short minutes, he would return with enough food to last for days.

But when he pulled himself up on the other side of the fence, Roscoe felt his stomach again. This time it flip-flopped in fear. In front of him were two furry legs. On top of those was a tall, furry body.

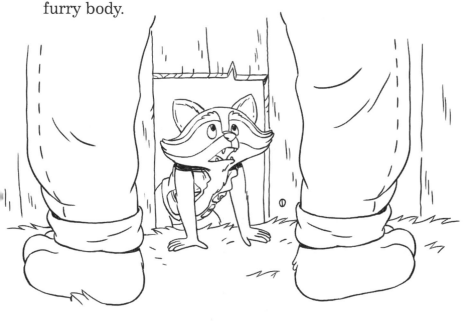

Roscoe blinked to make sure what he was seeing was real.

"Good morning!" he heard a squeaky voice say. It was not the sound he expected such a large animal to make.

Roscoe rubbed his eyes. He knew a bear when he saw one. But this one seemed to have a rather tall, pointy head. Roscoe took a deep breath, found his spectacles, and placed them near the tip of his snout.

The pointy part of the bear's head moved, and Roscoe saw that it had two legs of its own, along with two muddy red boots. It also had two wings and a beak.

"A—Are you wearing a woodpecker?" Roscoe summoned the courage to ask the bear.

"He's not wearing me," said the squeaky voice, which Roscoe could now see was coming from the bird. "I'm resting on him."

"I see," said Roscoe. "And who are you?"

"I'm Wanda. And this is Bartholomew."

"Everyone calls me Bart," the bear said with a yawn. "Bartholomew is too long a name." He slid a sticklike object from under his arm, which folded out into a type of chair.

"A hidden seat?" Roscoe asked, admiring the contraption.

Bart nodded. "I need to rest. We've been through a lot."

"That is an understatement," said a voice from behind a rock.

"Who's that?" Roscoe scratched his head. Fear had given way to total confusion. He was not used to visitors at his doorstep. And certainly not so early in the morning.

Out popped a badger. On her back was an overly stuffed green backpack. "I'm Luna," she said. She turned to the bear and the bird. "We've come this far. I refuse to give up."

"Come from where?" asked Roscoe.

"From Evergreen Valley, of course," Wanda said. "Don't you know what happened?"

"What?" Roscoe asked shyly. He did not care to mention how long the rain had kept him indoors.

"It started with the fire," said Bart. "It burned the trees and all the grass. We had to leave our homes."

"Oh my. Well, I am glad you are okay," said Roscoe. "Now, if you will excuse me, I was just on my way—"

"It isn't just the fire," Luna added. "With no roots to soak up the rain, it turned the earth to mud. The rain caused mudslides. Bart's cave—gone! Tree homes for Wanda—gone! Tunnel homes for me?"

"Let me guess," said Roscoe. "Gone?"

"Exactly," said Luna. "I can't dig in mud."

"So..." said Roscoe. "What brings you here?"

"We were hoping you could help us," Bart replied.

Roscoe suddenly felt nervous. Helping? That might mean sharing. Sharing might mean not enough for him. "H—How's that?" he asked.

"Well, for one thing," said Luna, "food! We are starving!"

9

"Food?" repeated Roscoe.

"Yes, food," said Wanda. She flew from her perch and landed on a branch near Roscoe's face. "*We* know that *you* know where there is food."

"How do you know all that?" Roscoe asked.

Wanda stuck out her chest. "Because," she said, "I have been watching you."

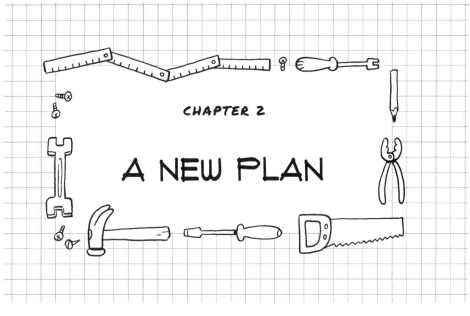

CHAPTER 2

A NEW PLAN

"You were...watching me?" Roscoe took off his spectacles and rubbed his eyes. "How on earth have you been doing that?"

"Is that a trick question?" Wanda spread out her wings. "What do you think these are for?"

Roscoe put his spectacles back on. "Well, I know that you're a bird, but...but..."

"I spotted you three days ago," Wanda continued. "You were munching away in that place across the river. Trust me, I'd fly there right now, but there is no way that I can carry all of the food

11

that Bart requires."

"We were wondering if you might have some food behind that big fence," said Bart. "It's pretty clear not much is growing on this side of the river."

"The sign says this is a junkyard," said Luna. "I'd even agree this once to eat junk food."

"It's not that kind of junk," said Roscoe. "And I ran out of food myself."

Wanda gave Roscoe a suspicious look.

"We all just want to find food," said Bart. "Wanda says we have a food source across the river. So enough talk." He adjusted his suspenders. "Let's get going."

"That sounds like a great plan," said Roscoe, turning to go back under the fence and into the junkyard. He didn't mind other animals reaching the dump before him, especially if it meant he could get back to his routine. Roscoe liked food as much as the next raccoon. But he loved his routine.

Before Roscoe could take a step, Luna called out, "Great! So you will help us?"

Help? When Roscoe said that it was a good plan, he had not meant he would go along! He turned around. His three visitors watched him hopefully.

Roscoe sighed. *I guess it won't hurt to show them to the crossing,* he thought. *Then I will have done a good thing, and getting back to my routine will feel even better.*

"Of course," he said. "Follow me."

So Roscoe led the way down the hill and to the grove of pines by the river. "I cross Big River here," he explained. "Up ahead are the rocks that I normally…"

Roscoe's voice trailed off. Nothing about what he saw was normal. The river's water moved faster than ever. The walls of the riverbank were overflowing.

"I've never seen the river like this," said Roscoe.

"It's due to the rain," said Wanda. "We've been trying to tell you about the flooding."

"This is the spot where I hop across the rocks to get to the other side," explained Roscoe. "Then I walk to the dump and—"

Roscoe was interrupted by his growling stomach. He put his hands on his belly and patted it gently. "Oh, calm down," he said.

"I am trying very hard to stay calm," Wanda replied.

"Sorry, I wasn't talking to you," Roscoe muttered. He didn't dare tell the others he often spoke to his stomach.

"I believe we need a new plan," said Luna.

Roscoe sighed. Luna was right. With the rocks underwater, he needed to find a new way to get the others across the river. The sooner he did that, the sooner his visitors could be on their way.

He took out his drawing pad. It was where he came up with his best plans. But as he stared at the empty page, no plans came.

Maybe I should sit down, Roscoe thought. When Roscoe would sit and take deep breaths, his ideas seemed to go from his brain to his drawing pad more easily. But as he sat next to a boulder above the riverbank, no new ideas came.

Roscoe slouched against the large stone.

Wait a minute! he thought. *Wasn't a boulder a first cousin to a rock? And rocks are what he jumped on to cross the river to get to his oh-so-delicious food!*

16

His brain worked quickly, and he drew furiously. All Roscoe had to do was push the stone down the bank and into the river. With such a large boulder, his visitors would then be able to cross. It was perfect! Roscoe set down his pad, stood up, and pushed with all his might against the boulder.

"What on earth are you doing?" asked Wanda. "Or, I should ask, why are you trying to *un*earth that boulder?"

Roscoe didn't answer. Not all of his ideas, drawn or otherwise, were successful. He could tell this was one of those times. "I was simply trying to find a way to cross the river by stepping on the boulder. Alas, it won't budge," he said at last.

"The first step to making a plan is to understand the problem." Luna unzipped her backpack. She took out a book and began flipping through the pages.

Bart opened his folding seat and sat down. "My brain works best when I am resting."

As Bart closed his eyes and Luna looked in her book, Wanda hovered next to Roscoe.

"While they think about that," she said, "I have a plan right now. And, Roscoe, it involves you."

Roscoe became nervous once again. "And what is that?" he asked.

"The rain washed away our habitats," said Wanda.

"Yes." Bart yawned. "We are in the habit of having habitats." He chuckled.

"Bad joke," said Wanda.

"Habitat?" asked Roscoe.

Luna looked up from her book. "Our environment—where we live."

"Exactly," said Wanda. "Roscoe, we need a place to live!"

"I see," said Roscoe. "How can I help with that?"

"That very large junkyard is your habitat," said Wanda. "I think you can put two and two together."

"Of course I can," said Roscoe. "Two and two makes four."

"That's right," said Bart. "The four of us, all together."

"Roscoe, the question is, can we depend on you?" asked Wanda.

Roscoe crossed his arms. "I will have you know I am very dependable."

"Good!" said Wanda. "Then it's settled. We'll stay with you in the junkyard."

Stay with Roscoe? How on earth had he agreed to that?

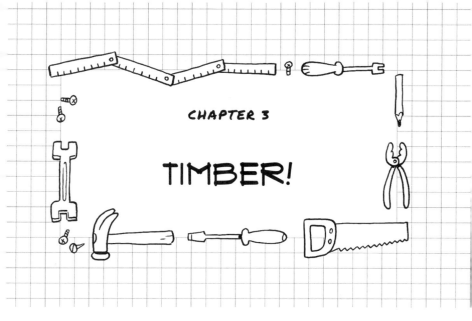

CHAPTER 3

TIMBER!

Wanda tapped her muddy red boot. "What do you say, Roscoe?"

Roscoe paused. Having visitors stay with him was *definitely* not part of his routine. But he did need to get across the river just as much as Bart, Luna, and Wanda did. And he was starting to think he might not be able to get there without them. "Well, just until we can get something to eat," he said.

"It's settled then!" Wanda cheered. "Let's get to work."

"Way ahead of you," said Luna, waving her book. "I've found just what we need to do."

"Eat?" said Roscoe.

"Well, yes," said Luna. "But to do that, we simply need to build a bridge."

"Simply build a bridge?" said Bart. "Now that's a bad joke."

Roscoe had to agree. He liked to make things, but he couldn't imagine building a bridge. Especially on an empty stomach. "That sounds… complicated," he said.

"It doesn't have to be," said Luna. "A bridge can be simple. It just needs to provide enough *force* to carry us across."

"Force?" asked Roscoe. The bridges he had seen had never forced anything. They just…sat there.

"That's right," said Luna. "Like your rocks in the river. You may not have realized it, but when you pushed down on them, they pushed back. They gave you force to get to the other side."

Roscoe had never thought of rocks like that. "So we need something that pushes back," he said, pacing along the riverbank. He stopped and leaned up against an old, dead tree. "Where will we find that?"

"I know!" Wanda called. "We can see what we have in our junkyard."

Our junkyard? thought Roscoe. "Now hold on a minute!" he said.

"Is something wrong, Roscoe?" Bart asked.

Roscoe did not want to sound rude. He picked at the bark of a tree. "Nothing is wrong," he said. "I just...I don't think the junkyard has anything we can use."

"We may not need the junkyard," said Luna. "Because Roscoe just gave me an idea."

"I did?" Roscoe scratched his head.

"You still are," said Luna. "We can use the very tree you're leaning on!"

Roscoe, Bart, and Wanda turned to the tree. "I'm looking at a very dead tree," said Roscoe.

"Exactly," said Luna. "Because the tree is dead, we can push it over. Then we can position it so that it goes from one bank to the other. The tree will be our bridge."

Then we can run to the dump to get food!
Roscoe thought. He quietly told his stomach, "I'll
feed you soon."

"Thank you for offering
to feed us, Roscoe," Luna
replied. "But once we're
at the dump, we can feed
ourselves."

Roscoe put his paw to
his face.

"I will supervise and
let Roscoe get to the root of
this tree-removal problem."
Bart chuckled.

"Bad joke and bad idea," said Wanda. "You're
the strongest, Bart. You and Roscoe need to work
together."

"All right then." Bart got up, folded his chair
seat, adjusted his suspenders, and stood opposite
Roscoe. The dead tree stood between them.

"One, two, three—PUSH!" Bart told Roscoe. They each pressed on their own side of the tree. Nothing happened.

"I'm certainly using all of my force," said Bart. "I don't know about Roscoe though."

"I'll have you know I'm using all my force!" said Roscoe.

Luna shook her head. "I fear that your approach is the problem," she said. "According to my book, every force has a direction. If you push

in opposite directions, each force works against the other. That tree won't budge."

"Oh," said Bart and Roscoe at the same time.

Bart moved to Roscoe's side.

"Good thing Luna and I are here," said Wanda. "Otherwise, you'd be lost."

"I will have you know I am not lost!" said Roscoe. "I've been on this riverbank many times."

"Please concentrate and push," said Luna.

Once the two were in position, Bart called, "Ready, set, push!"

Crack! The old tree toppled onto the ground.

"Well done!" cheered Luna.

"Now we need to get it to the edge of the riverbank," said Wanda. "Bart, that's a job for you."

"How about we give Bart some help?" said Roscoe. Even he was surprised at his offer to help.

"That's the spirit," said Luna, giving Roscoe a pat on the back.

But in the back of Roscoe's mind was his very own personal plan. If they were successful, he was sure the others could find a home by the dump. He'd have his home all to himself.

Once the animals were in position, Bart called, "One, two, three, tug!"

All at once, the group pulled on the tree, and all at once, the tree's branches dug into the ground. One by one, the animals slipped and fell. Luna landed on Bart, Roscoe landed on Luna, and Wanda landed on top of them all.

"The more we pull one way, the more the branches push the other," said Roscoe.

"That is called friction," said Luna. "It's the force that resists movement between two objects."

"Well, it's *forcing* us to try another approach," said Bart. "Let's try carrying it instead."

So, after brushing themselves off, Bart, Roscoe, and Luna hoisted the dead tree above their heads.

Wanda flew above them. "Down this way. A little to your right. Now to the left just an eensy-weensy bit. Too far!" she shouted.

"Make up your mind," said Bart.

"Perfect! Drop the tree here," said Wanda.

With a heave, they dropped the tree next to the riverbank. For a moment, no one spoke as they caught their breath.

"Now we just need to position the tree so it spans the river," Luna said finally.

"Easier said than done," said Roscoe, standing up. "But I'm ready. What about you Bart? Bart?"

Bart was not ready. He was lying on the ground with his head resting on the tree. And he was sound asleep.

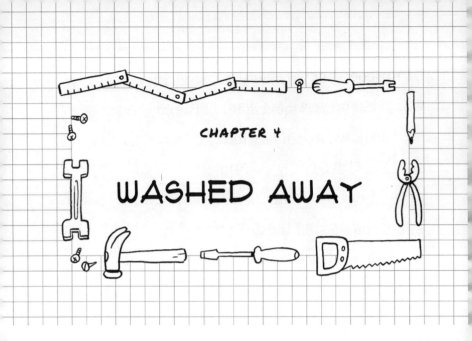

CHAPTER 4

WASHED AWAY

"Wake up!" Wanda's beak tapped gently on the top of Bart's head.

"Where am I?" Bart suddenly sat up.

"On one side of the riverbank," said Luna. "We want to be on the other. Which is why you need to get up."

"I remember." Bart stood and stretched. "Sleeping makes me forget my hunger."

"Maybe you forgot," said Roscoe. "But we are all hungry."

"What's that grumbling noise?" asked Wanda.

30

Roscoe knew exactly what that noise was. It was his stomach—grumbling and growling louder than ever. "Let's go, everyone!" he said, changing the subject. "We need to get this log across the river."

"How?" asked Bart.

"I think the best approach is this," said Luna. "We lift the tree straight up, aim it across the river, and let it fall onto the other side."

"This time, I'll supervise," said Roscoe.

"Well, since I can fly above you all, I should be the one to supervise," said Wanda. "Roscoe, you need to lift!"

So Bart, Luna, and Roscoe grabbed the tree by the top. Together, they tipped it into the air and got ready to drop it across the river.

"A little to the left," directed Wanda. "Get ready to drop it when I say…" Suddenly she flapped her

wings furiously. "WAIT! WAIT!" she called.

"I can't hold this tree much longer," said Roscoe.

"Let's drop it at the count of three," said Bart. "One, two, three!"

"I SAID WAIT!" Wanda called. "There's something coming down the river!"

"Oh dear," said Luna.

The tree smacked down on the other bank just as a log sped down the river. *Crash!* The speeding log slammed into the bridge. Before they knew it, their perfectly wonderful solution was swept away.

At first everyone was too shocked to speak.

"I can't believe it," Bart said at last. "I thought that tree would be our bridge."

"And after all that work!" Roscoe sighed. "Anyone have a plan now?"

"I have a suggestion," said Luna. "But I am hesitant to…"

"Well, I'm not hesitant," said Wanda. "Roscoe, we're going to your junkyard. There have got to be things we can use to build a bridge."

"I can lead the way," said Bart. "Follow me, friends."

Friends? Roscoe thought. *They were about to raid his home!*

Wanda was the first to reach the junkyard. She shook her head at the sight of the crawl space under the fence.

"Roscoe, is this how you go in and out?" she asked.

"Yes," said Roscoe. "I always come and go this way."

"Well," said Wanda, "we'll have to build a proper door for Bart and Luna."

"First things first," said Luna as she scrambled under the fence. "Building a bridge is our main goal."

Bart crouched down low and wiggled his way under the fence, followed by Roscoe. Wanda flew over the top.

"You won't like it here," said Roscoe. "It's got…"

"A tree for me!" cheered Wanda.

"A cave for me!" called Bart.

"A tunnel for me!" said Luna.

"What are you talking about?" Roscoe put on his spectacles to see what they were seeing.

"This coatrack makes a perfect tree," said Wanda.

"This metal hut makes a perfect cave," said Bart.

"And this underground storage space makes a perfect tunnel," said Luna.

"You must be joking," said Roscoe.

"We are not," said Wanda. "Well, friends…" She turned to the group. "I'm glad we found our new habitats."

Roscoe crossed his arms. A new door to his junkyard? New habitats for his visitors? He was starting to think things would never go back to normal.

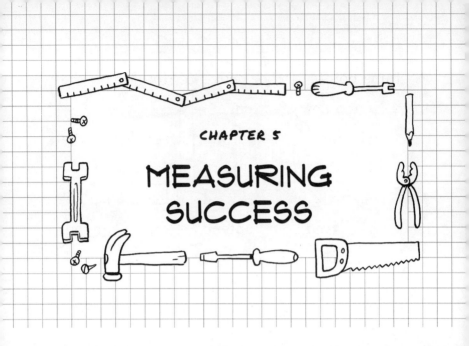

CHAPTER 5

MEASURING SUCCESS

Wanda perched in her new nest. Bart lay in his new cave. Roscoe slouched in his favorite armchair. The group's plan to make a bridge was starting to feel like Roscoe's plan to move that boulder: a dead end.

Luna stood at a table with her book open. "I refuse to give up," she said. "Our prototype may not have worked. But that does not mean it was a failure."

"Proto-what?" Bart called out. "Is that a fancy name for that dead tree?"

Luna pointed to her book. "A prototype is the first try at a new creation."

"Well, our prototype was swept down the river," said Bart. "I would call that a failure."

"It is only a failure if we don't learn from it," said Luna. "And I don't intend for that to happen. Let's make a list of what we learned. That way we won't make the same mistake on our next try."

Next try? thought Roscoe. He had been ready to give up on building bridges. But Luna seemed determined, and so far, she seemed to know what she was doing. Roscoe took out his drawing pad, spectacles, and a pencil, and joined her at the table.

"First, let's go over what went right," Luna said.

"Something went right?" asked Wanda.

"Oh yes!" said Luna. "Our bridge made it to the other side of the river, after all."

"That's right," said Bart. "The tree was long enough to reach the other side."

"Our next try will need to be just as long," said Luna.

Roscoe wrote down *Bridge must be long.*

"What about what went wrong?" asked Luna.

Bart stretched his arms as he walked over to the table. "That old tree was heavy," he said.

Roscoe nodded. "We definitely learned that. There's no way we could have carried it from the junkyard."

On his list, Roscoe wrote down *Bridge must be light.*

"What else?" asked Luna.

"Uh, hello!" said Wanda, flying down from her perch. "The bridge went down the river!"

Roscoe scratched his head. "How do we solve

that problem?"

Luna borrowed Roscoe's pad and pencil. She drew two curvy lines with squiggles in between. Roscoe could see that was the river. Then she drew two lines across the river. Roscoe could tell that was their tree bridge.

"Our bridge would have stayed put," said Luna, pointing to the lines across the river. "Except…"

She drew a skinny rectangle with an arrow going toward the bridge.

"The log," said Bart.

Luna nodded. "When it hit the bridge, there wasn't anything on the other side pushing back. It pushed the bridge in another direction."

"Downstream," said Wanda.

"Exactly," said Luna. "We need to build the bridge high enough so no other force can push it out of the way."

Roscoe wrote *Bridge must be higher*.

41

Wanda scanned his list. "So we need something that is light, long, and up high," she said.

The group set out through the junkyard. Wanda flew above. Roscoe, Luna, and Bart walked below. They passed bathtubs and stoves, cabinets and window shutters. They found hammers, saws, nails, and rope. There were many supplies, but none seemed right for their project.

Roscoe, Luna, and Bart came to a place with ladders leaning against a tall pile of scrap metal.

"These ladders are tall," said Roscoe. "From the top of the metal pile, we will be able to see more of the junkyard."

"And if we need to, we can move them and search other places," said Bart.

Bart placed his feet on the first rung of the ladder, but before he could start to climb, Wanda landed above him.

"I've found what we need," said Wanda. "But you will need to take your feet off that ladder first."

"Why is that?" said Bart.

"Because we cannot carry our bridge with you on top!" said Wanda.

Roscoe looked down at his drawing pad. They needed something *long* and *light*. "Wanda's right," he said. "We can use ladders!"

Bart stepped back, and together they carried the ladders back to the draw-ing table. As they went, Luna picked up an electrical cord and wrapped it around her shoulder.

"If we put the ladders together, they should be long enough to get us across," Roscoe said.

"Excellent suggestion," said Luna. "But first we must—"

"Don't tell us we need another list," said Bart.

"No," she said. "Not a list. We need to measure the river where we plan to cross. That way we'll know how long to make our bridge."

"Luna's right," said Wanda. "But how are we going to measure it?"

"I don't think they make tape measures that big," said Roscoe.

"I don't believe we will need a tape measure," said Luna. "We need you, Wanda. You're the only one who can fly."

Bart scratched his ears. "How does Wanda being able to fly help us measure?"

Luna raised the coil of cord. "I will tell you on the way!"

"Ready!" Wanda said after the group arrived at the riverbank. They placed the cord on the ground away from the edge of the river. Wanda grabbed one end in her beak. In a flash, she was up, up, and away.

"Get ready, Roscoe," Luna instructed. "As soon as Wanda is at the other side, we need you to mark the cord. That will give us an accurate measurement of the river."

Roscoe unzipped his pocket and took out his trusty blue marker. "Ready," he said.

At the other side of the river, Wanda hovered above the bank.

"Time for us to measure," said Bart.

"Mark the cord a little way away from the bank," said Luna.

Roscoe followed Luna's instructions. From that blue mark, the cord spanned clear across to the other side of the river. After Roscoe was done, they gave Wanda the signal to drop the cord and started pulling it back to their side.

"We did it!" said Bart.

"You can fly back, Wanda," shouted Roscoe.

But Wanda wasn't flying back. Instead, she was flying away, toward the dump. Was she leaving them behind?

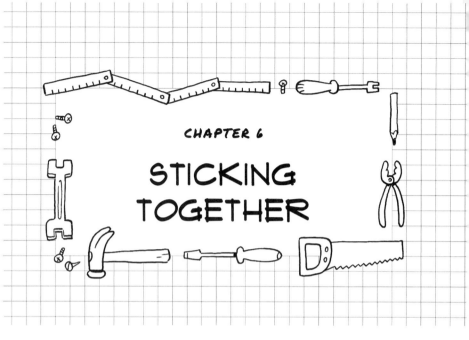

CHAPTER 6

STICKING TOGETHER

"I can't believe Wanda would abandon us," said Luna. "I will simply wait for her to return."

Sure enough, five minutes later, Wanda returned. She swooped down and landed gently on their side of the riverbank. She had a large, folded leaf in her beak.

When she set the leaf down, round, purple orbs fell out.

"I found some berries on the other side," said Wanda. "It's not a meal, but at least it's something."

Bart reached for some. "Thank you berry

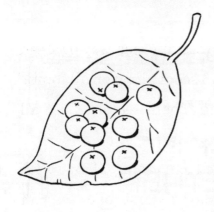

much," he said with a chuckle.

After Wanda had divided the food up, Roscoe gently placed a berry in his mouth. It wasn't tuna-pickle pizza, but it was food. He was starting to see one good thing about sharing.

Back at the junkyard, the four of them gathered around the drawing table with their ladders and measuring cord. Now they just needed to assemble their bridge.

"Wait a minute," said Bart. "Ladders have those wooden things."

"They are called rungs," said Luna.

"Whatever they are," said Bart. "When we put our bridge across the river, we can't stand on them. We might fall through the spaces in between." Bart looked down at his belly. "Well, I won't. But you all will."

"Wanda can fly across," said Luna. "For us

three, we can climb across another way. Instead of standing, we three can scoot along on all fours."

Bart chuckled. "I see. The three of us use all fours."

Roscoe found himself chuckling along. With food in his belly, even Bart's worst jokes weren't so bad. Together, the group measured each ladder.

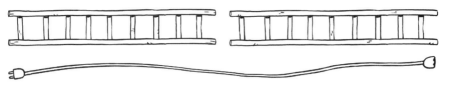

"I think two ladders will do it," said Bart.

"But how are we going to join these ladders together?" asked Wanda.

Luna looked up at Bart, Wanda, and Roscoe. "Oh my," she said. "I was so busy thinking about our list, I hadn't thought of that."

Bart opened his chair seat and slumped down. "Now what?" he asked.

Roscoe's good mood started to fade. Was all their hard work going to be for nothing?

After a deep breath, Luna was back to work. "I'm sure I can find a solution." She took out a book from her backpack. "We just need to do a bit of tinkering."

"What does that mean?" said Roscoe.

"Tinkering," said Luna, "means trying things out to see what happens. If we tinker enough, we can solve any problem eventually."

Roscoe liked the sound of solving problems. But he didn't know if his stomach could wait until *eventually*. He rummaged through boxes by the drawing table. There had to be something to use in order to attach the ladders. They needed something just as hard as wood, or even harder.

Roscoe came across a can of screws. The screws were just like the ones that held his wooden drawing table together. "What about these?" he asked.

"Yes," said Wanda. She picked up a metal strip with holes in it. "I bet the holes are for the screws

you found, Roscoe. I'll use my beak to peck holes into the ladder so we can screw them in easier."

"Wonderful," said Luna. "We can screw those metal braces to each ladder's side rail. That will give us one strong bridge!"

"We are back in business," said Bart. He flipped up his seat and began collecting metal braces.

"I'll collect the screws to go in those holes," said Roscoe. "Bart, you're the strongest. You should be the one to screw them in."

That is exactly what they did. Once the supplies were gathered, Luna held the braces in place, Wanda pecked out holes, and Bart screwed in the screws. They placed two braces on the outside of each rail and two braces on the inside.

"Our bridge is long and light," said Wanda. "We are ready to go!"

"Not yet," said Luna. "There's one more item on our list."

Roscoe took his drawing pad out of his vest pocket. "'The bridge must be above the river,'" he read.

"Oh yeah..." said Wanda. "How do we do that?"

Luna held up a wooden block. "We need to attach one of these to each corner. That way, the bridge will sit high enough above the water."

Once they were done, the group lifted the ladder bridge and headed toward the river. But when they got to the fence, there was one more problem.

"The only way out is the crawl space," said Luna. "There's no way we can shove this bridge through there."

"I don't believe it." Bart shook his head. "Will we be stopped because we have no door to the outside—just a silly crawl space?"

"I have an idea," said Roscoe. Without thinking

twice, he grabbed a hammer from the workbench and banged out two of the wooden slats in the junkyard fence. "We now have a door," he said with a smile.

Together, they grabbed hold of their very long ladder and marched through.

"Thanks, friend," Bart said as they headed for the river.

Friend. Roscoe was starting to like the sound of that word.

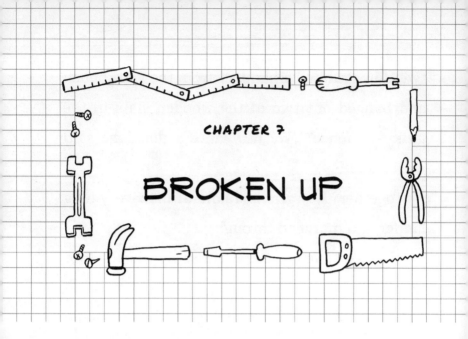

CHAPTER 7

BROKEN UP

"One, two, three—DROP!" Wanda called from above. Below, Luna, Roscoe, and Bart let their ladder bridge drop across the river.

Whooooosh! The ladder sailed through the air.

"I can't look," said Wanda.

"You can look!" cheered Luna. "It landed!"

"It landed smack on the other side of the river," said Bart. "And just like you wanted, Luna. It's above the riverbank!"

"Well done!" said Roscoe as he patted his belly. Now that he thought about it, he wasn't talking to his belly as much. He certainly hadn't forgotten his hunger, but he'd been busy working with the others.

"Luna, you should go first," said Roscoe. "It was your plan. We couldn't have done it without you."

"Well, if you insist," she said.

"I'll meet you all on the other side," Wanda said as she flew off.

Luna crouched on all fours. She scooted onto the ladder. She grabbed a rung and moved a tiny bit forward. She grabbed the next rung and moved a step forward. Inch by inch she started to cross the river.

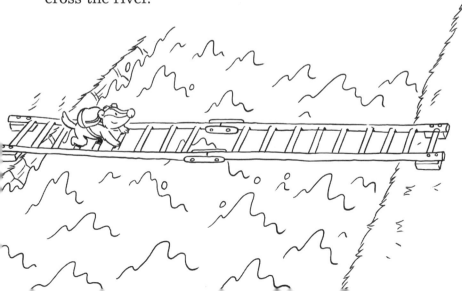

"I can't believe we've actually done it!" said
Bart.

Creeeek, crack, craaaack! Where was that
noise coming from? In seconds, they knew.

"Help!" cried Luna. They watched in horror as
she slipped. She held onto the ladder's side rail,
but her legs dangled just inches above the river.

"Hold on!" shouted Bart. He turned to Roscoe. "You need to climb out to get her."

"Me?" said Roscoe. He didn't just dislike rainstorms. He disliked anything that had to do with water. But there was Luna—stranded! He had to swallow his fear and try to save her.

"Those rungs won't hold if I go," said Bart.

So Bart steadied the end of the bridge, and Roscoe slowly started to inch his way along the edge of the ladder.

"Hold on, Luna!" Bart said over the roar of the river.

Roscoe felt his heart beating a mile a minute as he got to her. Carefully he reached out.

"Got you!" he cried as he grabbed Luna's backpack and pulled her up.

Slowly, the two crawled back along the edge of the ladder. Wanda flew nearby, encouraging them.

On shore, everyone collapsed against the giant rock. No one spoke for the longest time. Luna was the first one to say something.

"I am so very sorry," she cried. "I am a terrible planner and a worse tinkerer. I should have tested the rungs on that ladder. I didn't realize some of them were rotten. As I made my way along, a rung snapped in two the second I touched it. Then the others began cracking."

"It's not your fault," said Wanda.

"I agree," said Bart. "Nevertheless, we are back where we began." He let out a groan.

"Roscoe, you are very quiet," said Wanda.

"I'm thinking," he said. "Luna's ladder idea was great."

"No, it wasn't." Luna sighed. "I failed. I failed you all."

Roscoe stood up. "It's only a failure if we

don't learn from it. Isn't that what you said about tinkering?"

Luna smiled. She dried her tears and stood up. "Thank you, Roscoe. You're right. We need to keep trying."

Bart and Wanda weren't so convinced.

"It's getting dark," said Wanda. "I will fly to the riverbank and get some more berries, but I think after that, we should call it a day."

"We tried our best," said Bart.

"We can't give up," said Roscoe. "I'm sure we can come up with another idea."

"Sadly, I cannot eat ideas," said Bart. "Maybe Luna and Wanda and I should be on our way."

"I think Bart may be right," said Wanda. "We may have better luck finding food if we split up."

Split up? Not work together? Not even be together? The thought made Roscoe's stomach tighten. And it wasn't from hunger.

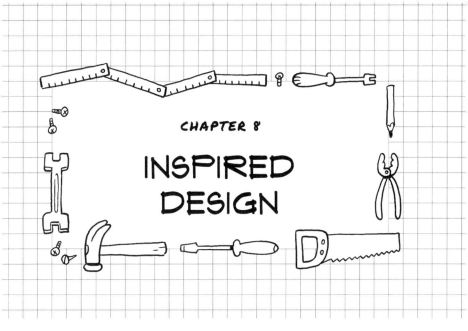

CHAPTER 8

INSPIRED DESIGN

"Maybe we need to take a moment to think," Luna said. "We are all hungry and tired. It has been a very, very long day."

"Tired, yes. But I can do something about our hunger," Wanda said. She opened another leaf filled with berries.

"Before I make my decision to go or stay, I will nap in my cave." Bart popped some berries into his mouth, then headed for the metal hut.

"Before I decide, I will nap in my tree." Wanda flew to the coatrack.

"Well, my motto is 'Never give up,'" said Luna.

Roscoe nodded. He didn't want to give up either.

"Then that leaves the two of us to come up with a plan," said Luna. She unzipped her backpack, found the right book, and leafed through the section about different kinds of bridges.

Roscoe took a walk around the junkyard. He thought about how the old objects were once used and how they worked. Often times, doing so sparked an idea for one of Roscoe's projects. He passed by bathtubs and stoves, cabinets and window shutters. He found hammers, saws, nails, and rope.

He looked at his list. They needed to make something *long* and *light*. Roscoe added another point to his list. They also needed to make something *strong*.

After a short walk, he hurried back to the drawing table and sat next to Luna. They sat quietly as they each wrote down their ideas.

After a while, Luna and Roscoe cheered at the same time.

"This is it!" said Luna.

"I've got it!" said Roscoe.

He held up his drawing. "We can use window shutters!" he said.

"We can make a suspension bridge!" said Luna.

They each looked at each other's drawings. They looked the same!

"Let's hope this plan will get Bart and Wanda to stay," said Luna.

When the four of them gathered together, Luna used their drawings to explain each step. "The shutters we use will be strong and light," she explained. "They are too thin to attach with our metal brackets. But we can connect them with rope to make them long enough to cross the river."

"Hold it! Hold it!" said Bart. "I'm not doing one more thing until we are sure that the wooden shutters will hold us."

"Good thinking," said Wanda.

"Bart, we need you to stand on a shutter," said Roscoe. "If it holds you, it will hold the rest of us."

They placed a shutter between two chairs. Bart stood on top.

"Jump up and down," said Wanda.

"I'll jump *and* sing and dance," said Bart. "If this works, you won't be able to shutter me up." He chuckled. Then he tested the other shutters.

"That was a good joke," said Wanda. "After we cross the river, we can *all* dance. Well, the shutters seem strong enough. But now what?"

"We weave the ropes in and out of the shutter slats to lash them together," said Luna. "That's how the shutters will stay together."

"But this bridge bends," said Wanda, looking at the picture Luna had drawn. "If we put it on the riverbank, it will dip into the water."

Luna pointed to each end of the bridge on the drawing. "Unlike our last bridge, this one won't sit on the riverbank. We will tie it to the boulder on our side. The other side will connect to the berry tree across the river. From there, it will hang over the river."

Bart cut in. "I can tie square knots."

Everyone looked at Bart in surprise.

"What?" he said. "I learned from watching campers."

"Wonderful!" said Luna. "Wanda, we need your help too. You found the tree on the other side of the river. Your job is to secure a pair of ropes around that tree."

"Hmm." Bart scratched his ears. "It sounds good but..."

"I know what Bart means," said Wanda. "It works in your pictures, but we've had so many disappointments. I can't handle any more."

Luna looked up at the rising moon. "Maybe we should get some sleep first," she said. "If you agree to stay, we can try it first thing in the morning."

Bart and Wanda looked at the drawings. They looked at each other and nodded. "Okay," they agreed. "We'll try out one more plan."

So Luna headed for her tunnel, Bart to his cave, Wanda to her tree, and Roscoe to his shed. Roscoe's stomach growled as he climbed into his cozy, warm bed. But as he lay under the covers, he decided to draw one more picture in his drawing pad, for good luck. Then he fell asleep, hoping his drawing would become a reality.

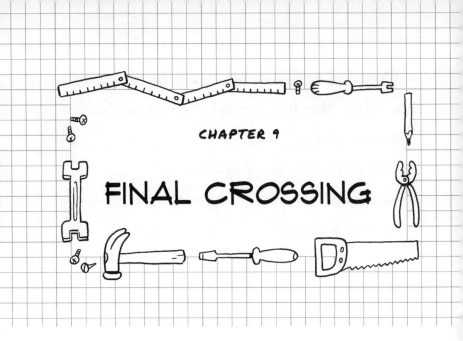

CHAPTER 9

FINAL CROSSING

Early the next morning, Roscoe woke as the sun poured through his shed's window. He took it as a good sign.

The four tinkerers got to work. Bart insisted on retesting each shutter. Then they lined their shutters up end to end and weaved a rope through the shutter slats—first weaving one side, then the other. Their shutter bridge grew longer and longer.

Wanda found their measuring cord. She flew it over the strung-together shutters. Yes! Their shutter bridge was long enough to span the river.

"Now it's time to measure our rope endings," said Luna. "One pair needs to be twice as long as the river crossing."

"Why so long?" asked Wanda.

Luna pointed to Roscoe's drawing. "Those ropes have to reach the tree on the opposite bank *and* be long enough to get back to our side."

Roscoe wasn't sure he understood that part. But too much rope was never a bad idea, and he trusted Luna knew what she was doing.

After working all morning, the group was ready to bring their bridge to the river.

Bart found a wheelbarrow in his cave. So they folded the shutters into the wheelbarrow and carefully placed the pair of long rope ends on top.

"Roscoe, why not tell us what kind of food we'll soon be eating," said Bart as they

headed for the river.

"One never knows what one can find," said Roscoe. "But it's usually delicious." He pictured tuna-and-pickle pizza, his favorite.

At the river, Roscoe, Bart, and Luna carefully lifted their shutter bridge out from the wheelbarrow and rested it on the ground. Then Bart and Roscoe found the shorter pair of rope endings. They wrapped them several times around the giant rock.

"Watch this," said Bart. "Right over left. Left over right. That's a square knot. It's sure to hold."

"Your job is next." Luna handed Wanda one of the very long rope ends from the other side of their shutter bridge. "This piece of rope is coming from the shutter's right side. Bring it around the tree going from right to left. Make sure it rests above a branch so it won't slip."

"Got it!" said Wanda and put the rope end in her beak.

"Then fly that rope end right back to us!" added Luna.

Wanda flew off. When she returned, she gave the rope end to Bart. "Now I bet I'm supposed to bring this left rope end around the tree going from left to right and give it to Roscoe," she said before she flew off.

"Exactly," said Luna.

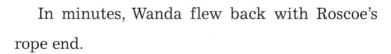

In minutes, Wanda flew back with Roscoe's rope end.

"Now you must pull with all of your might," said Luna.

Now Roscoe understood why the rope endings

had to be so long. Instead of dropping the bridge across the river, they were going to use the ropes to pull it across!

"This just might work!" said Wanda.

"I know it will work," Luna said. "But I am afraid to look." She covered one eye.

"One, two, three, pull!" Bart directed. He and Roscoe pulled and pulled. The coils of rope piled up around them, and the bridge began to move, ever so slowly. First it scraped along the riverbank.

"It's heading for the river," said Wanda. "Now I can't look."

Luna joined in to help Roscoe. They had no choice. They had to look to keep pulling on the rope. Paw over paw, each one kept yanking away. With each tug, the shutter bridge inched closer and closer to the river's edge.

"Yes!" they cheered. "Our bridge is going across and *above* the river!"

"Keep pulling," said Wanda. "It's working!"

After a little while, Bart said, "We can't pull any more."

"That's because we've done it!" cheered Luna. "Now let's tie your ropes to the boulder and cross our bridge."

After the ropes were tied off, Wanda, Bart, Roscoe, and Luna did a victory dance. Then they hopped onto their beautiful wood-shutter suspension bridge.

"Don't you want to fly over?" Roscoe asked Wanda.

"Are you kidding? After all this work, I'm walking too," Wanda said as her red boots clicked across the shutters.

Once everyone had reached the other side, Roscoe led the way to the dump. It seemed much closer than it had felt.

"Here it is!" Roscoe said as he pressed open the gate. "Welcome to our food source."

Roscoe dove in, searching for his favorites. He

found an apple core and a banana peel—a slice of pizza! It was a bit soggy, but he didn't mind.

"Isn't this wonderful?" Roscoe called to the others.

But there was no answer.

Roscoe looked up. Luna, Roscoe, and Wanda were nowhere to be seen. Had they left him alone? After all that?

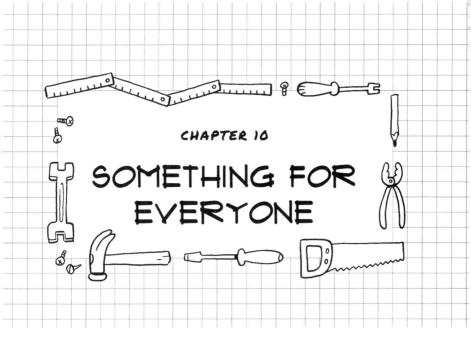

CHAPTER 10

SOMETHING FOR EVERYONE

"Over here!" someone called. It was Bart's voice, but it was coming from outside the dump. What on earth was he doing there?

With food in his belly and pizza in his hand, Roscoe followed the voice past the fence. He had never thought to travel beyond the dump before.

On the other side was a field filled with grasses, leaves of every shape and size, piles of nuts, and flowers of every color of the rainbow.

"Sorry to leave you behind," said Luna. "But we found this wonderful field."

Bart was munching on a berry-nut medley. Luna was mixing a flower and herb stew. Wanda was eating an acorn and dandelion-root salad.

"You are missing the best food!" said Roscoe.

"That may be the best food for you," said Wanda. "But not us."

"We are used to a different kind of diet," said Luna.

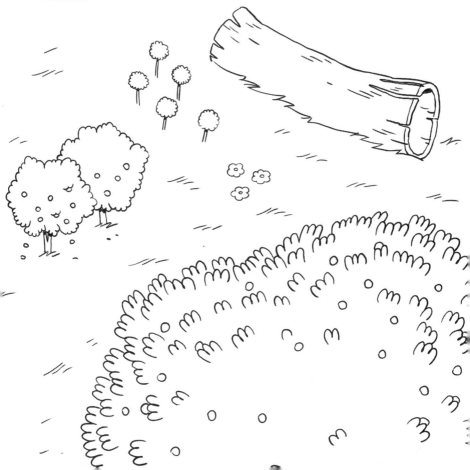

"Here there's something for everyone," said Bart. "Even for you." Bart held out a handful of berries from a bush.

Roscoe had not thought that his friends might not like pickle-and-tuna pizza. And he wasn't so sure he wanted to try new foods. But he had learned a lot during his time with the others. He decided to give it a try.

Roscoe plopped a berry into his mouth. It was good! He sprinkled some more on his pizza. Even better!

"What's that noise?" Wanda asked after she finished her meal.

For the first time, Roscoe admitted it. "That's my stomach. It talks to me, and I talk to it."

Wanda rested her head on Roscoe's belly. "I hear it too," she said. "Your stomach is saying 'Good food!'"

Roscoe broke into a huge grin. As much as he liked his routine, he decided he liked trying new things even more. Who knew what new creations they could make?

Once they had all eaten their fill, Roscoe said, "Now that we've found our food, I hope you will stay."

"We talked about that very question before you arrived," said Wanda.

"We agreed to stay under one condition," said Bart.

Roscoe became nervous.

"We absolutely must make a proper door for that junkyard," Luna explained.

Roscoe smiled. "I will help make our door. And I have something to add to it, as well," he said.

Roscoe unzipped his vest and pulled out the drawing he had made the night before. He showed it to the others.

It was picture of four friends: Bart, Wanda, Luna, and Roscoe. And above them, in big, rainbow-colored letters, were the words *Home of the Tinkerers*.

THE DESIGN PROCESS

It can take a lot of creativity to build a solution to a problem. By following the engineering design process, the Tinkerers make sure they are putting their creative ideas to good use.

STEP 1 Figure out the problem

Every engineering project begins with a problem that needs to be solved. For example, the Tinkerers need to figure out a way to get across the river safely.

STEP 2 Design a possible solution

The next step is to come up with an idea for solving the problem. Luna proposes they try building a bridge.

STEP 3 Build and test a prototype

The Tinkerers' first prototype is a big tree, which they plan to lay across the river.

STEP 4 Evaluate the prototype's performance

The tree bridge doesn't work. The water's current causes a log to smash into it. From this, the Tinkerers learn that their bridge needs to be higher above the river.

STEP 5 Present the results

Engineers take knowledge from each prototype and go back to Step 1. After their first prototype, the Tinkerers work on solving their new problem by designing a bridge that sits above the river.

FORCES AT WORK

A force is an action that affects an object's motion in some way. One force we feel all the time is gravity. It pushes down toward Earth, keeping us from floating away. The Tinkerers notice the force of gravity when they try to lift a big dead tree. Gravity makes it heavy!

Another common force is friction. It occurs when two objects are touching. When the Tinkerers try to drag their tree, friction between the tree and the ground makes it hard to move.

All forces follow certain rules. In 1686, scientist Isaac Newton presented three laws that outline the ways forces work:

1. The first law says that if an object is at rest or moving at a constant speed, it will stay that way unless another force acts upon it. This is called *inertia*. The inertia of the log floating down Big River is so powerful that it knocks the Tinkerers' first bridge out of place.

2. Newton's second law says that a force will cause an object to accelerate, or change speed, in the same direction as the force. The greater an object's mass, the harder it is to change its speed. When Roscoe tries to push a giant boulder into the river, he can't apply enough force to move it.

Also, forces can add up or cancel each other out. When Bart and Roscoe push toward each other from opposite sides of the tree, it doesn't move. The forces cancel out. But when Roscoe and Bart push in the same direction, the forces add up. The tree falls right over.

3. The third law states that for every action, there is an equal and opposite reaction. This means if

you apply a force to something, that thing will also apply a force to you. When Bart, Roscoe, and Luna pull on the rope to position their bridge, they find out that it is hard work. This is because the rope is also pulling back against them.